EXPLORE
my
world

Lions

Amy Sky Koster

NATIONAL GEOGRAPHIC KiDS

WASHINGTON, D.C.

A lion!

He strides across the grassy plains on big, padded paws. Looking and listening, he keeps watch as he roams.

He wanders over rocks and lounges by a water hole. He huddles low to wait out a sudden rain.

The long fur around a lion's head and neck is called a mane. Only male lions grow manes.

Roar!

This lion's job is to protect his family and their space.

When lions from other families get too close, he roars loudly. It warns "Keep out!"

The lion's roar also wakes his family from a nap. They yawn and stretch. They grunt and growl as he joins them.

Lions are the only wild cats that live in family groups.

Lion families are called prides. A pride usually has two or three males and several females and their cubs.

It's time for the females to gather dinner for the pride. Mothers, daughters, and sisters team up to hunt big animals.

They roam from dusk to dawn, on the lookout for prey.

Water holes are great places to catch food. But watch out for crocodiles!

wildebeest

Pounce!

A lion sneaks up on her prey. She dashes at it from her hiding place.

What will today's meal be? Wildebeest? Zebra? Gazelle?

gazelle

Female lions are fierce hunters, but they are tender mothers.

A mother lion hides her newborn cubs in the bushes. To move one, she carries it gently in her mouth.

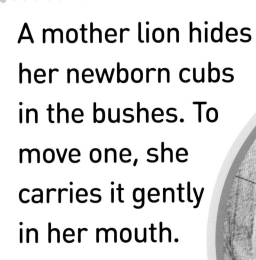

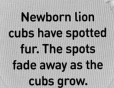

Newborn lion cubs have spotted fur. The spots fade away as the cubs grow.

A mother
lion licks her
cubs clean with
her tongue.
She feeds them
with her milk.

18

She shows her cubs everything they need to know to survive in the wild.

Playtime!

Just like you, growing cubs love to play. They play with sticks— and tails!

They clamber over their mothers and other adults in the pride.

Cubs chase, leap, pounce, and bite. They tumble and tussle in the grass.

22

Playing is more than just fun for little lions. It also teaches them how to hunt and how to defend themselves.

23

Snore!

After all of that roaming, roaring, hunting, pouncing, and playing, it's time for another nap. The pride snuggles together in the grass. Sleep well, lions!

Built to Hunt

Female lions do most of the hunting for a pride. They hunt large animals such as wildebeests and zebras, and smaller animals such as warthogs and gazelles. Here are a few things that help lions chase and catch the food they eat.

FUR
The color of its fur helps a lion blend in with tall grass as it waits for its food to come closer.

TAIL
Its long tail helps a lion stay balanced as it runs and leaps.

BACK LEGS
The lion's long back legs help it jump.

The lion is the only big cat with a tuft of fur at the end of its tail.

How many other wild cats can you name?

EYES
Its eyes can see movement far away. Lions can also see well at night.

JAWS
Powerful jaws and long, sharp teeth help lions grab hold of food.

FEET
Padded feet help a lion creep up quietly on its food.

CLAWS
Sharp claws snag and grip prey.

How quietly can you walk?

Roars and More

Lions growl, snarl, hiss, and grunt to talk to each other, but they are famous for their earsplitting roars. A lion's roar can be heard up to five miles (8 km) away. Here are a few more animals—some of them quite tiny—that can really raise a racket.

The tiny **BUSH CRICKET'S** chirp can be as loud as a power saw.

OILBIRDS are the loudest birds. They live and shriek and squawk in caves.

A **HOWLER MONKEY'S** call can be heard up to three miles (5 km) away.

The **BLUE WHALE** is the loudest mammal of all. Its underwater song can be heard more than 500 miles (805 km) away.

When **COQUI FROGS** call together, they can be as noisy as a lawn mower.

Can you name some other loud animals?

How loud a noise can you make?

Can you name some quiet animals?

Home of the Lion

Lions live in parts of Africa and Asia.

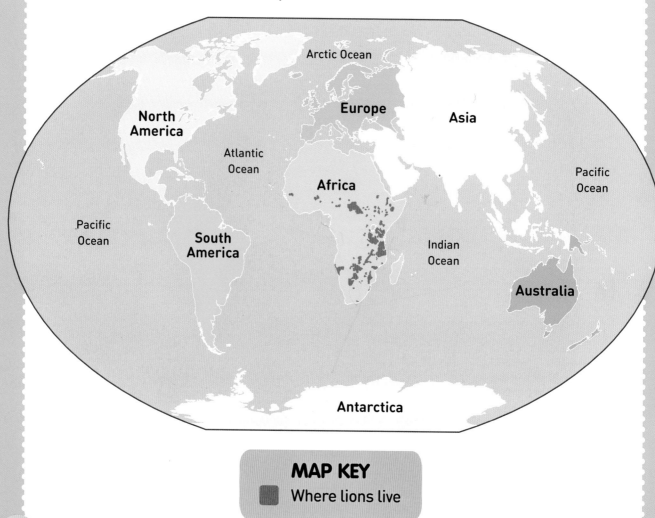

Arctic Ocean

Europe

Asia

North America

Atlantic Ocean

Pacific Ocean

Africa

Pacific Ocean

South America

Indian Ocean

Australia

Antarctica

MAP KEY

Where lions live

Name That Family!

Lions live in family groups called prides. Here are some other animals that live in groups with special names. Can you match the animals with the name of their group?

POD   HERD   PACK   TROOP

_____ of monkeys

_____ of elephants

_____ of wolves

_____ of dolphins

To my lion —A.S.K.

Since 1888, the National Geographic Society has funded more than 12,000 research, exploration, and preservation projects around the world. The Society receives funds from National Geographic Partners, LLC, funded in part by your purchase. A portion of the proceeds from this book supports this vital work. To learn more, visit natgeo.com/info.

NATIONAL GEOGRAPHIC and Yellow Border Design are trademarks of the National Geographic Society, used under license.

Library of Congress Cataloging-in-Publication Data

Names: Koster, Amy Sky, author. | National Geographic Society (U.S.)
Title: Lions / by Amy Sky Koster.
Description: Washington, D.C. : National Geographic Kids, [2018] | Series: Explore my world | Audience: Ages 3-7. | Audience: Pre-school, excluding K.
Identifiers: LCCN 2017018191 (print) | LCCN 2017031379 (ebook) | ISBN 9781426329906 (e-book) | ISBN 9781426329883 (pbk.) | ISBN 9781426329890 (hardcover)
Subjects: LCSH: Lion--Juvenile literature. | Lion--Pictorial works.
Classification: LCC QL737.C23 (ebook) | LCC QL737.C23 K67 2018 (print) | DDC 599.757--dc23
LC record available at https://lccn.loc.gov/2017018191

Designed by Sanjida Rashid

The publisher gratefully acknowledges Dr. Craig Packer, Director, Lion Research Center, University of Minnesota, for his expert review of this book.

Printed in Hong Kong
17/THK/1

ILLUSTRATIONS CREDITS

Front cover, Andy Rouse/Minden Pictures; back cover, Eric Isselée/Shutterstock; 1, amrishw/Shutterstock; 2-3, Paul Souders/Getty Images; 4-5, Maggy Meyer/Shutterstock; 6 (UP), Michael Nichols/National Geographic Creative; 6 (LO), Sergey Uryadnikov/Shutterstock; 7, Denis-Huot/Nature Picture Library; 8, Volodymyr Burdiak/Shutterstock; 9, Uwe Skrzypczak/imageBROKER/Alamy; 10 (LE), Sicha69/Getty Images; 10 (RT), Julian W/Shutterstock; 11, David Griffin/National Geographic Creative; 12, Anup Shah/Getty Images; 13 (UP), Jeff Mauritzen; 13 (LO), Alexander Sviridov/Shutterstock; 14 (UP), Travel Stock/Shutterstock; 14 (LO), Stuart G Porter/Shutterstock; 14-15, Mogens Trolle/Dreamstime; 16, Maggy Meyer/Shutterstock; 17, WLDavies/Getty Images; 18 (UP), steveblloom.com/Barcroft Media/Getty Images; 18 (LO), Chris Minihane/Getty Images; 19, jez_bennett/Getty Images; 20, Anup Shah/Minden Pictures; 21, MHGALLERY/Getty Images; 22 (UP), Anup Shah/Nature Picture Library; 22 (LO), André Gilden/Alamy; 23-25, Michael Nichols/National Geographic Creative; 26-27, GlobalP/Getty Images; 27 (INSET), Dirk94025/Getty Images; 28 (LE), FLPA/Alamy; 28 (RT), Dr. Natasha Mhatre; 29 (UP LE), eco2drew/Getty Images; 29 (UP RT), Juan Carlos Muñoz/Getty Images; 29 (LO), Maresa Pryor/National Geographic Creative; 31 (UP LE), gnomeandi/Getty Images; 31 (UP RT), Jonathan Pledger/Shutterstock; 31 (LO LE), Alan Jeffery/Getty Images; 31 (LO RT), Daniel McCoulloch/DV/Getty Images; 32, Arturo de Frias/Shutterstock